A Battleaxe and a Metal Arm 19:

Motes of Death

Samuel Fleming

Thank you to my Beta Readers

And, as always, to my First Reader,

Mel.

Contents

"Death is not a tragedy.
Giving up is."

—*Unfettered*

Previously…

A desert of glass gave way to a realm of shadow, ash, and death. Helesys pushed aside the darkness with her warding light, but they would wander toward the heart of Sala Gahenna—the dungeon—in near darkness.

They walked across the ashen beach for miles. Soon, they were set upon by serpents, simple made-things, that converged en masse upon them. Helesys held the serpents, then commanded them to die. Instead of psychic recoil, she felt nothing.

This gave her pause. Shouldn't it pain her to snuff out the life of another… even if those things were not truly alive?

Son, they came to the edge of land and the edge of a churning black sea. With the water walk spell, they pressed out onto the hills and waves. Their unease grew the closer they pressed to the center of the realm.

Slender sharks came for them, and the heroes met them with magic blasts and steel. They cleaved and broke the beasts—the weapon, the vessel, the wisp.

Soon a bellow shook the realm. Through the sullen crests, a gargantuan silhouette appeared. A serpent rose from the sea and stretched up to the sky before turning toward them. Taunauk leapt into battle, blazing golden. Shawn and his poison dagger were close behind, but the serpent dove beneath the waves. It tried to ambush them from below, but Helesys rained arcane blasts down on it before Taunauk split it in half with his ancestral power.

But calling on so much power left Taunauk weak, and other Endroggen helped carry his body. His father, Rehkoros, walked beside them for a while. He reassured them, and confided in Helesys both about his son and about her potential to learn Endroggen blood magic.

Next, they came to blackened dunes, littered with remnants of long-dead creatures—things half-digested by the realm. Purple clouds grew like a another rolling sea. And from the sky, a meteor fell—

A three-headed dragon made of shadow and darkness. It turned toward the heroes, and attacked with lightning and black-serpents. Helesys made short work of the latter while her allies attacked. She tried to hold the beast, but instead found that it was a primordial god. Helesys defended against the beast's lightning while Taunauk and Shawn attacked.

When it unleashed its lightning, Helesys coalesced the spell on her, drawing in and channeling its destructive power, then redirecting it back at the dragon. Her blast struck true, and the black dragon retreated into the sky. But Helesys and Taunauk were spent from using their magics.

The walked wearily across the dunes of glass and came to a canyon that cut across the landscape—one small part of a massive scar in the realm. After a brief respite, they continued along the canyon ridge, before being ambushed once again by the black dragon. Again she coalesced lightning on herself, this time just enough to spare her comrades.

They came to the cliff's end with nowhere else to turn. Just when the dragon was about to strike them down, a massive hand reached up from the darkness, breaking the dragon.

A titan rose from the scar—the kin of the Dungeon, of the Gatekeeper, of the Queen. They learned that the scar was the birthplace of the Queen. That she was both the dungeon and the master of—the marble and the sculptor. In the end, the heroes leapt onto the jade lemur and fled the titan, maiming it with the curse of cold fire.

And when the titan begged the Queen for aid, she laughed at her kin.

The heroes flew away toward the center of the scar. It was there that they found the well, the hole in the realm. They were sucked in like a whirlpool and plunged into darkness. Remnants of creatures attacked them and Helesys struck them down with a word.

Then the world vanished.

~ ~ ~

Fitful Sleep

Helesys sat on the edge of her mother's bed, running her fingers over the edges of a hairbrush. It was carved from crimsonwood, from one of the last ancient trees felled before the elves retreated inside Novissimé. Before they gave up the outside world.

It *was* beautiful.

Helesys often came to her mother's bedroom to think. To procrastinate. To escape.

This time, she had come from history class. Helesys was destined to lead Great House Byyra one day, and the years weighed on her even though she was a child. The city of Novissimé loomed large through her mother's window. Helesys was caught between thousands of years written in stone and an uncertain future. All the while standing in the ominous shadow of the unwinnable Eternal War.

There was an elegant metal spear laying on the bed—had that been there the whole time?

"You always were an old soul."

Helesys looked up from the brush and saw her mother, Wynbella, standing in the doorway. She still looked strong, not as frail as after father's passing. Not as frail as she did during Helesys's last days in the city.

Young Helesys wanted nothing but to go to her, to throw her arms around her mother, to break down. To weep.

A *child* wanted that… but Helesys wasn't a child. The hands that hold the brush were far too large—one was gleaming metal. She was a spellweaver, a soldier.

Helesys knew her mother wasn't real.

There's something powerful in that, isn't there? said another voice from the edge of the room… No one was there. *Something primal in seeing your mother again. Something you understood even when you were shattered and broken after your death on the Eternal Battlefield.*

"I know that voice…" Helesys said, her eyes searching the room.

"Of course you do," Wynbella replied. She's still standing in the doorway. Poised and regal. How she looked before father passed.

Realization dawned on Helesys—her wand was the other voice. "But you left me."

I never left, Helesys. I was always there. Always a part of you.

"So why can I hear you now?" Helesys turned to her mother. "Why do I see you now?"

Wynbella asked, "Does it matter?"

"Of course it does."

"Would it be so bad if this was just a fond memory or a comforting dream? To know you can keep coming back to it?"

Tears welled up in Helesys's eyes and she fought them back. "It would make it worse."

Yes, it would, her wand said. *You keep coming back to a past you can never return to.*

Wynbella asked, "Where are you, Helesys, if not in this room at this very moment?"

"I…" Helesys stopped, breath caught in her throat as she looked around the room. She walked to the window and looked out over the spires of Novissimé and the mountain slopes beyond.

It wasn't real—Helesys had to remind herself of that—because it *looked so very real.* Just like her mother. Helesys couldn't trust her eyes. Clearly, that was the answer.

Helesys backed away from the window. Heart pounding. She kindled power without thinking. Anything to push back against the despair closing in on her.

It was a pitiful comfort.

"What's wrong?" Wynbella asked.

Helesys's breath was ragged, even with kindled power. "I—can't breathe."

Wynbella walked over and rested a hand on Helesys's shoulder. For a moment, her breath relaxed. Helesys turned to her mother, pleading without speaking, but refusing to embrace her.

Her mother wasn't real. Home wasn't real.

"This isn't real," Helesys muttered. "I don't know where I am… I don't know you."

Wynbella's face softened, "You never knew me, Helesys."

"…What?"

"How could you? You died," Wynbella said. "You left before you could… before you trusted me again."

Helesys shook her head. "I—I didn't… I left because I wasn't whole. I didn't remember anything. I didn't know who you were. I didn't know *who I was.*"

"You died. You should've stayed with me and let me take care of you until you'd mended." Wynbella reached for her hands, but Helesys pulled away.

"This isn't—this isn't real!" Helesys clenched her fists. She turned—

"You're leaving again, just like last time."

Helesys stopped, mid-stride. Her eyes fell to the floor. "Yes."

"I loved you," her mother said, voice quivering. "I loved you, no matter what."

Helesys looked up and found a man leaning against the doorway. He wore leather armor with hood pulled over to hide his face. His face was deeply tan, that of a Terran, though his features were as sharp as an elf's. His eyes were a piercing blue. Black bandages wrapped his hands.

"I'm sorry to interrupt—"

"Do I know you?" Helesys asked.

His eyes wrinkled and, for a moment, he wore the same pained expression as Wynbella—disbelief of being forgotten by one held so dear.

"I'm Shawn. You're right that this place isn't real."

"I know."

"*I am* though."

Helesys eyed him cautiously, power still flickering in her arm. He was different—more than Terran... and more than the pale shadows of memory that surrounded her.

Finally, she said, "I believe you. What is this place?"

Shawn rapped his knuckles on the doorframe. "It's a dreamscape, of sorts. We were on the King's path, heading toward the center of the Dungeon. Do you remember?"

Helesys nodded slowly. It was coming back to her slower than she liked, but it *was* coming back.

"Most realms in the dungeon were physical planes—the castle, the endless sea, the underground—but we've gone past that point. We're close to the center. Before there were realms and before the Queen was born, there were dreams. That's where we are now."

"Whose dream is this? Whose dream are we in?" Helesys demanded.

"Yours," Shawn replied. "But not just yours. Mine are here too. Taunauk is here somewhere. The King's memories are likely here… and so are the Queen's."

Helesys shuddered at the thought of the Wolf King and the Queen, but nodded to Shawn's explanation.

"Let's go," she said, glancing back. Wynbella still stood beside the bed, hands clasped, waiting nervously.

"Do you need a minute?"

"No."

Shawn looked from Wynbella and back to Helesys. "This isn't a bad place, Helesys… Memories can be a weight or they can be a blessing… For Movernus's sake, *hug your mother.*"

Helesys needed no further urging. She turned and embraced her mother. Her chest quivered with sobs until she felt like a child in her arms.

"I love you, no matter what," Wynbella said.

In that moment, Helesys didn't care what was real and what wasn't. Holding her mother was what she needed.

~

Sometime later, when Helesys's eyes burned and were bereft of tears, she grabbed the spear from the bed, and left without saying goodbye. She couldn't say anything—Helesys swore she would survive, win her freedom, and journey home to tell Wynbella herself. To tell her mother that she was sorry and that she loved her.

Helesys and Shawn walked abreast through the halls of Novissimé, each step calling forth memories of the dungeon—

And memories of home.

Memories that aren't yours.

Helesys passed her father's study that was always locked, the storage cupboards where Aradi would hide when skipping class, and two separate libraries where she'd spent countless evenings.

None of it real.

None of it her.

Shawn must've read her face. He frowned. "I'm sorry. Wading through memories isn't something most mortals are used to. And this place… is strange. They aren't *perfect* memories. More like echoes of the past. But still, they are closer to the truth than we'd like to admit."

They turned a corner in the long stone halls and stopped suddenly. A dozen guards stood at the end of the hall, all wearing the smooth polished plate mail of the royal guard.

The Princeps stepped to the front, hand on the hilt of his sword. "Helesys, we've been asked to escort you back to your room." His face was weathered and wrinkled, and he looked at her with a mix of sternness and apprehension.

Helesys knew him—she might have known *all* of the royal guard since she was a child. But she couldn't recall his name.

"I'm leaving," Helesys said, stepping forward defiantly, "and you are in my way."

The Princeps shook his head. "You're not well. Please—"

"No." Her heart was pounding. She knew what came next.

Guards in the rear asked for orders. Guards in the front drew their swords. Helesys didn't stop walking.

The Princeps slapped the sword-hand of the man nearest. "For Movernus's sake, don't hurt her!"

Beside her, Shawn grabbed her wrist. "Helesys, are you sure you want to—"

She yanked her hand away with bolstered strength. "I already did this."

Guards shoved the Princeps aside, lunging past him to get to Helesys. The first tried to grab her, Helesys swung with her right arm and punched him in the face. His helmet caved in around her metal hand and he fell limp to the ground.

For a few whirlwind seconds, the hallway was like a drunken, violent brawl. Helesys shoved and battered her way through the guards, slamming them against the wall or toppling over one another. Their mithral armor screeched as it twisted around her blows, punctuated by the crack of bones, and screams of the men.

Only Helesys remained on her feet, surrounded by broken guards.

Shawn stepped past them and laid a hand on her shoulder. "It's okay."

"It's not okay," Helesys replied. She turned back and looked at the damage she'd wrought. Most of the men groaned in pain, clutching arms or legs. One had a metal arm like Helesys's—snapped in half. Three were dead, including the Princeps… She didn't even remember hitting him.

You did this.

"I did this," she said. "The day I escaped—the day I ran away. I killed them. It wasn't even a battle. It was slaughter— like killing an unarmed prisoner."

"It wasn't your fault."

He's right. You didn't even have the words to explain how broken and lost you felt.

Helesys pulled away from him. "A drunkard kills a man in a bar, it's still his fault! Shawn… I did this."

Are you even the same person anymore?

Shawn sighed. "I still say your situation is a *little bit* different. But you can't take it back. The only way out of this is forward. So, are you ready?"

One of the guards looked up at her from the ground, fear in his eyes. Helesys turned away in shame.

You didn't really want to remember.

She knew them—that was the hardest part. She knew everyone she hurt that day.

~

Helesys and Shawn ran through the halls of Great House Byyra. They avoided and outran two more groups of guards. Rather than go down the main stairwell, Helesys led them to the auxiliary stairs. Their footfalls echoed across the empty stone until they were near the bottom of the Great House.

And Helesys came face to face with her sister, Aradi. A twisted mirror of Helesys's own face that had haunted Helesys her whole life. .

Aradi's face turned into a sneer. "Where do you think you're going?"

Helesys stared her down from the top of the stairs. Shawn stood at her back.

"You know where. I'm leaving."

"But why?" Aradi feigned shock, like a serpent coiling before a strike.

Helesys took a step forward on the stairs. "You told me where Sala Gahenna is. What did you think would happen? I'm going."

Aradi's face twisted into a smile and she stepped to the side. "Good. Don't waste any time."

Helesys descended the stairs and stood inches from her sister. "You're manipulating me. I felt it then… but I *know* it now."

"How could you accuse me of such things?"

"My whole life, you've played games. It's what you do. I don't know you—I don't think I ever did."

Aradi smiled again, and whispered, "Who are they going to believe… me, or the crazy *machinervus*?"

Her memory of that day bled into the illusion, and Helesys wanted nothing more than to throttle her sister.

It had been easy to kill the guards. Far too easy… But now—and then—Helesys couldn't bring herself to harm her sister. The one person who had tormented Helesys her whole life.

Misplaced love—that's what it was. Somehow, after so much of her had been stripped away, Helesys both hated and loved her sister.

Helesys sneered and walked past her sister, leaving the agonizing memory. Shawn followed close behind.

"I don't like her," Shawn said, shivering. "Her name is too close to the mother of demons."

Ariazi… Your mother said she didn't care what it meant. She thought it was pretty.

Helesys replied, "It's a fitting name… Are dreams always this painful?"

Shawn shrugged. "What's worse, to be startled out of a nightmare or yanked out of salvation? Dread to sleep or dread to wake?"

~

They stepped out of Great House Byyra and onto one of the many stone bridges. A half dozen such bridges connected to an open air garden situated between the towers.

The sun nearly bowled her over for they hadn't seen a risen sun since their imprisonment—she smiled in spite of it. Behind her, Shawn muttered in exasperation. They crossed to the garden, and Helesys felt the pain of past memories pushed aside.

Shawn asked, "This is a good memory, isn't it?"

"Yes," Helesys replied, only half-listening. She walked through the terraces of flowers, running her metal hand over synthaeas that hung like strands of silver bells, mertleblooms that flickered in the sunlight, deep red roses, cat's ears, and dozens of others Helesys could never have named.

"Which memory?" Shawn asked from the row across from her. Despite the garden all around, he looked at her with a schoolboy's curiosity.

She chuckled. "The wisp is interested in memories now?"

"They're just dreams of another sort."

The honesty in his reply made Helesys pause, and she replied in kind. "I came here often. This place was my respite."

As she walked the terraces and rows of hanging flowers, Helesys was at once a child, adolescent, and young woman. The garden had meant many things to her over the years, but always one thing most of all:

In a towering city of stone and metal and glass, these scant gardens were an escape. Both nature and solitude.

There was a private garden in House Byyra, but there she could be easily found and hounded about studies or training. She much preferred the open air between the towers.

"Did you have anywhere like this?" Helesys asked. "A place in the dream world... or in ours?"

Shawn cradled a yellow blossom in his fingers and looked at it longingly. "I was a wisp. I had many… Then I had only one. That's why I became Terran." He let go of the flower and met her eyes. "I suspect we'll see it before long."

"Will you be ready for that?"

Shawn met her eyes with a fleeting smile. "I'll have to be."

Shouts echoed behind them, followed by the sound of dozens of metal boots on the stone. Helesys turned and saw guards spilling out of the Great House. More guards came from the other spires—converging on the garden. Moments later, they were surrounded.

A guard from House Byyra stepped forward, magical armor glistening in the sunlight. "Helesys Byyra, we are under orders to bring you home. Do not resist, or we will use force."

Helesys stepped to the front of the garden and stared them down, a defiant smile curling on her lips. Back then, she had been angry and desperate. But now… she knew what came next.

"Do you trust me?" she asked.

"Are you talking to me or to the guards?" Shawn replied.

Helesys met her friend's eyes. "Do you trust me?"

"Yes."

Helesys turned to the short wall that marked the edge of the stone walkway and leapt over it. Wind whipped through her hair as she plummeted through Novissimé to the walkways below.

~ ~ ~

The Border of Dreams

Helesys was falling. Shawn was right behind her, hooting like a madman.

The next stone walkway rushed up at them—impossibly small against the towering stone of the elven city.

Helesys bolstered her strength for the landing. She crashed through several wooden shelves, smashing flower pots and vases, hit the ground and rolled—knocking over two more rows. Only one table remained unmarred, and Shawn broke it a moment later.

"You're absolutely mad!" Shawn cackled, slipping on the rubble as he stood.

Helesys ran and leapt over the side of the walkway again. Wind whipped through her hair and she heard Shawn falling behind her.

But as she watched the stones of Novissimé rush by, she saw flashes of other realms: The rolling black waves of the ashen sea, lightning and hail above the Godpeak. Sandstorms covering long abandoned cities, the murky waters of the infinite sea flooding through cracks in the realm and into underground temples and crypts. Floating mountains, moving paintings, buried labyrinths, emerald plains, and finally the castle—the titanic obsidian face of it, jagged peaks skewering the clouds.

"Helesys!"

Shawn's voice brought her out of the trance. She tucked her legs just in time, hit the ground, and rolled painfully across it. She stood and found herself in a courtyard. Surrounded. Hundreds of startled elves stared at her. A few backed away. Some stared at her arm.

"It's her!" someone shouted. The crowd churned.

No one stayed to gawk at the fallen heir of Byyra. They all ran, jostling each other, shoving some to the ground. Helesys couldn't look away. She had never seen such fear—not even when the Shadowkind had broken their ranks on the Eternal Battlefield.

Shawn landed softly and was beside her a moment later. "Helesys," he said. He grabbed her arm. "Where next?"

Helesys didn't respond. She ran. Shawn followed.

She led them through the courtyard that threaded between the towering stone houses, down stairs that lead from level to level. Down they fled, away from the heights of safety that Helesys had known all her life. Down toward the mechanical bowels of Novissimé and the rest of the world that lay at the mountain's feet.

Guards gathered on the street below. Helesys turned and ran for the nearest doorway—ringed by symbols in the old words: *Systems* and *sewers*.

She slammed into the door. The metal hinges creaked under the impact, but held fast. Without understanding what she was doing, Helesys wordlessly unraveled the locking spell on the door. The second time she pushed, the door swung upon violently.

"In here," she said, before slamming the door shut behind her and Shawn.

~

As the door shut, darkness closed in around them—pushed aside quickly by lights along the ceiling. These passageways were bored into the mountain itself with a mix of drills, lathes, and magic. The resulting mix was a tunnel with porous floors for grip and drainage, while the walls and ceiling were edged and followed the natural rock lines.

Helesys and Shawn ran through the tunnels, spiraling deeper into the mountain.

They passed workers and shoved aside others—gruff men and women smeared with grease and arcane powders. Some cursed them. Some looked like grisly mirrors of Helesys, with metal arms or metal legs. But theirs were smooth, without the gruesome curves on her clawed gauntlet.

They passed junctions that led to refineries and smitheries, to pipe forges, and ancient catacombs of their elders. Clangs of pistons and shouts of the old words echoed along the stone. The air was thick with steam and smelled of metal and spice.

"I know you know where you're going," Shawn said over her shoulder, "but how did you know the way the first time?"

I know the way, her wand said. *Aradi made sure I did.*

"My sister," Helesys sneered. "My wand has blueprints to the city."

"So, she helped you escape?"

"Yes."

Shawn snorted. "Why, in Tamir's name, would she do that?"

Helesys paused at a junction. One way led to the sewers, which were completely blocked off by the refinery. One passage led to smitheries and ultimately to a dead end. From here, they needed to go to right—back out to the streets and through the main gate. With any luck, the soldiers had followed her into the passageways and hadn't expected a noble like her to make it this far through the undercity.

Helesys glanced back at Shawn. "My sister wanted me gone. I have no idea why, but I need to find out."

They took off running again, through the final stretches. When they came to the door, again Helesys unraveled the wards and pushed through.

They should've emerged onto the street and into the light. Instead, Helesys and Shawn found themselves in another passage—one dark and ominous. The lights behind them on the ceiling flickered and died.

In the darkness came a skittering and scraping, like iron nails on stone.

Helesys kindled her warding light and swept aside the darkness.

Creatures snarled in the harsh light, their voices a cacophony of wet and guttural voices. The closest was a twisted mass of bone and folded flesh that looked like it might slough off the joints. Its face stretched into a serpent's yawn, revealing jagged teeth that glistened in the light. The long body stood on several spider-like legs, but even these were split into fractals—the ends looking something like tree branches and threads of webbing.

Behind it, creatures even more twisted lurched—faces split open like grisly flowers, ribs protruded into limbs.

Power churned in her wand-arm. "This isn't—"

"Isn't how you remember it," Shawn finished. "I know."

No longer confused by the light, the creatures lunged for them, their bone limbs scraping on the stone.

Helesys grit her teeth and built the power till it rattled her gauntlet, then she fired. Purple power careened through the hall. The parts of the creatures that weren't outright vaporized splattered chunks and gore against the walls. Destroyed as easily as Helesys brushed aside the darkness.

But more twisted screams echoed through the halls—even from behind them, where no monsters should've been.

"I don't know where to go," Helesys whispered.

"Trust yourself. Physical directions won't help you," Shawn replied, and chuckled uneasily. "*You* go first. I'll watch your back."

Helesys smirked and stalked forward, power kindling in her wand and bolstering her body.

Creatures spilled into the passageway, drawn to either sound or gore. Helesys blasted them or broke them with her spear. Behind her, she heard Shawn doing the same.

Vaguely human faces lunged for her, and as Helesys destroyed them, she thought of the ratmen from the tunnels. She reached out to the creature's minds, seeking to end the fight quickly.

But when she entered their mindspace, instead of towering over the creatures like she had the ratmen, the creatures towered over her. Even with her might, Helesys was surrounded by legs as tall as ironwoods and jagged teeth that stretched like lightning across the sky.

Horrified, she ceased the spell and continued fighting in the hall. Helesys fought through the tunnels, slaughtering for every step forward while Shawn guarded their back. The damned creatures gave them no respite, and the heroes gave them no mercy.

~

By the time Helesys found the next door, the pair were soaked in blood. It was plain metal instead of stone, and unwarded. But when she pushed, it held firmly in place, metal groaning against her shoulder.

Behind her, Shawn's blades flashed against still more creatures and his cloak trailed with ghostly power.

Helesys bolstered her strength, then compounded it further with the Gar of Shéslang. Her breath swelled with strength and her bones grew heavy. Helesys leaned her shoulder into the door and *pushed*.

The lock snapped and the door swung open wide—slamming into the wall behind it. The hinges groaned and the door fell to the ground.

Helesys stepped through and the world grew hot. Steam filled the air and through it, Helesys saw bright molten slag. It fell in streams from the floors above and pooled in cauldrons and vats littering the floor. Along the ceiling high above, everlit candles loomed like stars. Clangs of smithing hammers and metal presses rang out like gongs.

This was no elven forge—it was a forge of men. The same one that Shawn had spent his mortal years in.

Helesys looked back and found the metal door remade—closed and locked in place. There were no more horrid screams.

Beside her, Shawn looked over the room. "Guess we're in my memory now."

Shawn took a step, but Helesys grabbed his arm. "Shawn, what were those things back there? Where were we? Were those people?"

Shawn nodded. "They used to be."

"I thought they were like the ratmen, but… they were something else."

Shawn said, "I've seen them before. They're *animissai*—lost souls. They're mortals who strayed too close to something they shouldn't have. In the realm of dreams, that's usually Nimicus or the rapax. But here… We're so close to the heart of the dungeon. Those *things* were probably Chosen. They've been usurped by the dungeon, by the Queen."

Helesys thought back to the mindspace where the creatures had towered over her—just like other ancient and eldritch monsters. She shivered at the thought of having been so close to the Queen.

Somehow that was worse—that even a fragment of the Queen's power was too much to comprehend, let alone stand against.

Shawn continued, "It happens in the mortal world, too. The Qwuikkach, the scourge of the druids, are made the same way…" Shawn met Helesys's eyes and trailed off. "There are things we were not meant to see."

"Is that why you left the realm of dreams?"

Helesys regretted the question even as it left her lips.

Shawn struggled to hold her gaze. "Yeah. I think it was." He shrugged. "Definitely a part of it."

"When we stand in front of the Wolf King, just… don't run away."

"Not on your life," Shawn replied. He turned from Helesys and walked through the factory. Helesys followed.

They passed by vats of molten metal that glowed with impossible heat. Helesys kindled strength as she stepped to the edge and peered into the cauldron. Liquid fire rolled within and even with strength, the chemical fumes stung her nose.

Helesys stepped back, taking in the factory with new eyes. "You don't use magic to control the process?"

"No."

"...Nor protect the workers?"

At that, Shawn chuckled. "They don't see us as people. We were just another link in the chain. Another spoke in the wheel."

Helesys looked over the workers that filled the room, faces smeared with soot and sweat. Were they so different from the underclasses that labored beneath Novissimé? They didn't look it, but at least the elves were protected. They didn't breathe caustic gasses and risk grievous injury or death… At least not within the confines of the city. The Eternal Battlefield was another matter.

Shawn read the conflict on her face. "It is the way of things," he offered.

"You could change things," Helesys replied.

"Could I?" Shawn leaned against a pillar. "What could I do? Destroy this place? They would rebuild it. Unite the workers? Give them dreams? There's nowhere else left to work and they won't leave. Not for all the gold in the next city."

Helesys was about to speak, but stopped herself. She saw the weariness on Shawn's face. It was the look of a man that wanted to help, but was powerless against the tide. It reminded her of the Eternal War and all the lives ground up just so they could keep the war at a stalemate… and how powerless she'd felt in the wake of it.

All she said was, "We are not the same as when we were first trapped here. Perhaps when we escape, we can set things right."

Shawn nodded. "Perhaps."

~

Shawn led them through the factory.

He walked with purpose, and at first, Helesys thought it was that danger might lurk in the corners of the memory. But as they walked further and further into the sweltering darkness, Helesys saw his gaze linger on workers.

Shawn never said who they were, never truly let her into his memory, and she didn't ask.

When a Terran had so little, it didn't feel right to pry the silence—the little solace they had left.

It was difficult, though, for twice when Helesys looked into the crowd of workers, she saw Shawn's own face staring back—soot-covered, and tired to the bone. Each time, the visage looked from Shawn to Helesys, and stared at her as they passed.

Helesys didn't know how much time passed, but eventually they stopped in front of tall stone doors. Elven script wrapped around it.

Helesys stepped forward, erased the wards, and pushed open the door.

~

Light poured through the door, and Helesys and Shawn stepped out into blinding sun. Helesys shielded her eyes, and saw a courtyard—

They were surrounded. A hundred soldiers stood in formation in a semicircle facing them. They all wore the gleaming armor of Novissimé. Their weapons drawn. Eyes cold.

By the time Helesys's eyes adjust, and she sees the full breadth of the soldiers, she knows there is no hope. No way for her to make it past all of them. Even though her hands were clenched in anger, not even the satisfying thought of taking so many with her is enough to move the weaver.

The Great Doors of Novissimé loom just beyond the shining blockade of soldiers. In that moment, the dark metal reminds her of the colossal face of the castle—the dungeon. Her home, her birthplace, mocks her.

A voice cut through the silence. "Let her go."

Slowly, the mass of soldiers lowered their weapons and stepped back.

Wynbella stood alone in front of the doors.

Helesys walked in stunned silence, until her and Shawn stopped in front of Wynbella.

"You let me go?" Helesys asked.

Wynbella nodded. "There was no other way." Then she turned to Shawn. "Take care of her. I beg you."

Shawn's eyes widened in surprise.

Helesys asked, "What is it?"

"I was there," Shawn said. "This happened… I came to Novissimé. I was mortal and searching for Sala Gahenna—for a way to ascend again. I used the last of my power to dreamsurf and find the elves that knew where the dungeon was.

"Your mother didn't want to let you go, but when you heard there was a wisp searching for the same forgotten place, you escape. You fought your way through the guards and down here. This is where we met for the first time."

Shawn's story triggered her memory, and Helesys knew it was the truth.

Wynbella said to Shawn, "There is an outlander at the gates, searching for the same. Take him to Sala Gahenna as well." She turned to Helesys, eyes glistening. "May you find everything you seek."

Helesys and Wynbella embraced, and Helesys hugged her mother tightly. She didn't let go, even when the heavy clangs of buried gears rang out, not when the ancient metal groaned. Helesys watched the doors with teary eyes.

When the Great Doors of Novissimé finally opened, Helesys ran through them and left everything she knew behind.

~ ~ ~

Lost

Helesys ran down the slope of the mountain at reckless speed. Her feet slid on the rocks, and she nearly fell down a ravine—

Helesys merely dug her metal fingers into the mountain to catch herself. Then she kept going.

She didn't stop until she was at the base of the mountain. Chest heaving, she stared out over the rolling hills of the countryside, the small human village, and forests that lay at the edge of the mountain.

Shawn came to a stop beside her, but neither spoke for a long moment.

Finally, Shawn said, "I'm sorry."

"About what?"

"About... all of that."

Helesys sighed. "It's not your fault. You didn't know. No one did."

Shawn chuckled. "I know that... It's not an apology, Helesys. I'm just sorry."

She nodded. "Yeah. Well, no happy Terrans go on an adventure like this, right?"

Shawn nodded meekly, then shrugged. "Could always be worse!"

Helesys stifled a laugh. "How in Movernus's name could this be worse?"

"We could be trapped in a lingering death and not even able to sulk about our suffering."

Helesys rolled her eyes. "Alright. Point taken. Let's find Taunauk and get on with this."

~

Helesys and Shawn entered the forest and soon lost sight of Novissimé—it wasn't just hidden behind the trees. Helesys knew that the space was gone and that there was no way out of the forest, save through it.

The trees rose up and up. Twisted limbs receded, giving way to towering trucks and a distant canopy. The smaller plants and grasses thinned until they died out completely.

They were in the Wode again, or at least a memory of it.

Helesys and Shawn walked with weapons ready and power kindled. They walked abreast.

Helesys asked, "Have you been here before?"

"No." Shawn's eyes flitted through the treeline, wary. "Must have gotten lucky. I think I'm glad."

Helesys thought back on Matron Mildé and her wolves, the Deacon and the village, and finally the Green Knight and her obsession with the Gatekeeper.

"It was one of our first realms," Helesys said. "Before we knew the truths of this place… Remember the black knight from the river of glass?"

Shawn chuckled. "Dreary? Kind of crazy?"

"The same. The knight… Well, she killed him. It was the only time we were separated by death. I kept going, kept walking. I tried to climb the infinite wall. I didn't make it."

"The name should've been a clue—infinite wall… Sorry. Bad joke. And every time you died, you both woke up together?"

Helesys nodded. "Every time."

Shawn sighed. "Perhaps we'll find out why I was by myself so often."

"But we kept finding each other," Helesys added, reassuringly.

Shawn smiled meekly. "Yeah. I would've rather stayed with you guys, though. Wandering alone isn't all it's cracked up to be."

"May you find the answers you seek."

Helesys meant the words with every bit of truth and reassurance, but they hung ominously in the silence of the Wode.

~

Time stretched on. The faint light that reached the forest floor turned orange and bleeding red, but set. Twilight hung around them, and for hours, they didn't see another soul nor hear birds or any life at all—

Not until wolves appeared in the distance. Three gray wolves stood completely still and stared at Helesys and Shawn. Their mouths hung open in hunger, and fur bristled on their backs.

Helesys kindled power. She aimed just above the nearest wolf and fired a warning shot. Purple energy soared across the Wode, twisting the silence, and passed just above the wolf's head. Close enough that it should've startled them, no matter whether they werebeast or Terran in disguise.

The wolves didn't move. They just stared. Unmoving.

Helesys thought back to the twisted creatures beneath Novissimé, of a nightmare that crawled into her memory.

More wolves stalked out from behind the trees—stopped and stared.

"Helesys…" Shawn whispered, looking to either side and behind them. "I don't think—"

The wolves began to writhe. Jagged bones broke through their skin as if their very skeletons were trying to escape. They split into half-human, half-grotesque faces like the creatures from before. In moments, they transformed into grisly spiders and skittered toward the heroes.

Shawn sighed and readied his twin daggers. "I hate it when I'm right."

Helesys called on her Ring of Winter and felt its cold power build within her. She turned to the left and shouted, *"Murum glaciei tempestatemque!"*

A wall of ice rose from the ground, fifty feet high, filling in the gaps between the giant trees. For a moment and only a moment, Helesys allowed herself a swell of pride. She'd come far since her first painful uses of the ring, and the journey had made her mighty.

With enemy forces divided, Helesys turned power inward and outward, bolstering her strength and her gauntlet, compounding it with the Gar of Shéslang. She fired repeatedly, sending blasts as large as Terrans across the Wode—shattering every twisted thing in their path.

The first wave of creatures was upon them—mindless bodies thumped dully against the wall of ice, nothing but vague shadows showing through.

Helesys and Shawn fought back-to-back. She turned spear and spreadblast against them with overwhelming force, swinging the spear so hard it became a cudgel and shots from her gauntlet exploded like blastshells. Meanwhile, Shawn became a hurricane of blades, a storm of death both everywhere and nowhere, all at once.

Enemies fell in droves, shredded and pulverized.

The terrible moment dragged on until Helesys and Shawn stood alone amongst the gore and the shadow of the ice wall. Her spear and gauntlet smoldered with steam. In mere moments, her breath relaxed and soreness had already left her muscles.

So easy, she thought.

It was always easy for you, her wand replied.

And as Helesys surveyed the carnage, memories came to her unbidden: The grisly dancer from Amadeus's tower, Dissimul from the machine realm, and the mirror image she fought in the King's gallery. All made-things, like her. Each had stared at her—recognized Helesys for what she was.

Is the weapon any different from the monster it slays? her wand asked.

She had always been a soldier, but now… she wasn't so sure.

Another memory came to her—this time the reassuring voice of Taunauk: *"The blade holds the warrior as much as she holds the blade."*

Shawn embraced her, and the two things brought her back to the moment. Hesitantly, she hugged him too.

"What was that for?" she asked.

Shawn released her and stood sheepishly. "You were doing that thing again. The thing where you stay off into space like you're talking to your wand but you have a horrified look on your face."

Helesys smiled, thankful for her comrades—her friends.

"Thanks," she said. "Come on, let's find Taunauk."

~

Twilight stretched on, but eventually, Helesys and Shawn came to a clearing in the titanic forest. A village sprawled across the clearing full of human men, women, and children. The canopy parted, casting the scene in a holy glow.

But the whole of it was eerily silent, and it wasn't until Helesys and Shawn entered the clearing and felt the sun that they heard anything at all—like they had found an island in a silent sea. Voices rose, but the Terrans paid no attention to the heroes.

They were Endroggen. Sun beaten faces, clad in furs and braids.

Helesys looked across the peaceful village, and imagined the people little different than her own.

She said, "They look so peaceful… it's hard to imagine them as a warrior people."

Shawn shrugged. "Every culture has their warriors, prophets, poets, and farmers. We only think it different because we know Taunauk."

Helesys smirked. "That is a fair point."

From across the village, cracks and clangs of battle rang out, and the pair walked toward it.

They walked between tents, passed racks of tanning skins, fletchers, and basket weavers. Children ran past them, laughing. They passed two fires with spits roasting over them—the smell of meat impossibly faint.

"It almost feels like an illusion," Helesys whispered.

Shawn muttered in agreement, then stopped suddenly.

Helesys followed his gaze and found a single man staring at them. He had the hard look of a warrior: Weathered face and cold eyes.

Helesys was sure she'd seen him before, and a look of recognition passed between them. His glare softened and became somber, and he finally looked away.

A voice from behind said, "We'd almost forgotten about you." They turned and found Rehkoros standing attentively. "It's good you've found us."

Helesys looked Taunauk's father up and down. The spirit always had a weary look about him—a father's worry—but he looked no worse.

"Where is he?"

Rehkoros looked slowly around at the village—not looking for his son, but taking in the sight of it. Respite was over.

Wordlessly, Rehkoros led them toward the back of the clearing. They walked around warriors sparring with sword, spear, and shield. Their long hair pulled back in ornate braids and wraps. Men and women that had been forged from iron.

It was only after they passed the sparring field that Helesys saw Taunauk. He was kneeling at the far edge of the treeline with his back to the village.

They walked over to Taunauk and found his eyes closed in meditation. He was the only Endroggen with his hair and beard shorn down to stubble.

Shawn asked, "Can... Can he hear us?"

"I can," Taunauk replied, eyes still closed.

"Oh. That's good," Shawn replied. "It's time to go, big guy."

"I am waiting."

Helesys asked, "For what?"

"I am waiting for the elders of Novissimé."

Helesys's brow wrinkled in confusion. Clearly, he was lost in a memory. Taunauk had come to Novissimé seeking Sala Gahenna just like Shawn had… But Helesys was no elder, and Shawn was not elven.

She asked, "What are you waiting for?"

"I am waiting for the elders of Novissimé to change their mind."

Realization dawned on her. Beside her, Shawn was shaking his head.

Helesys asked, "The elders turned you away, didn't they?"

"I am human. They are elven," Taunauk replied, eyes still closed. "They feel it is their right to refuse."

She asked, "And what do you believe?"

"I am the Vessel of my people, called to save the lost souls of Accaelum. My quest has echoed across time… I have faith that the elders of Novissimé will change their minds." Taunauk sighed. "For now, I wait."

Helesys and Shawn shared a concerned glance. Helesys asked, "Why do you wait here?"

"The fields remind me of home…" Taunauk's voice turned to a whisper. "I want nothing more than to go back."

Finally, Helesys said, "Taunauk, we're here. I think you were waiting for us."

Taunauk's eyes opened slowly, blazing with golden light. He looked tentatively at the forest, as if he hadn't opened his eyes in days.

"It's time, then," he said, and stood as if he was carrying the burden of an entire world.

Taunauk turned to face them, and as he did, the sounds of the village faded. Helesys watched as men, women, children, tents and campfires all vanished.

The only ones left were warriors, and they looked around the empty field with solace. Respite was over.

Slowly, Taunauk said, "I don't understand."

"This is a memory, Taunauk," Helesys said. "We already found Sala Gahenna. We're trapped inside. This place is an illusion, a trick to keep us from going further inside.

Bittersweet recognition passed over Taunauk's face as he locked eyes with his father.

"It's true, balac," Rehkoros said. "You've already found us. It is time to go."

"You can trust us," Shawn added. "It will come back to you."

Taunauk nodded. "It already is. I remember." He walked and hugged his father. And when they released one another, the rest of the warriors in the clearing faded into golden mist. The shimmering cloud returned to Taunauk.

Then he turned back toward the forest, head hung low in reverence.

Shawn said, "You can take a minute, if you need it."

Taunauk shook his head. "It reminds me too much of home, and that's not what I need right now."

~

They left the clearing and walked through the memory of the Wode. Shawn explained the strange realm to Taunauk— the twisting of memory, place, and the lack of direction.

"This place is confusing," Shawn added. "Malevolently confusing."

Taunauk said, "So we are going to Sala Gahenna again? But we've already gone inside?"

Shawn chuckled. "Yes, it is a conundrum. This place is more like a dreamscape than anything you would understand. We aren't traveling geologically, so much as metaphorically. We are going to the heart of the dungeon… Which also looks like we're going back to the beginning."

Taunauk glanced sidelong at Shawn. "Puzzling indeed."

Silence dragged on and it was a long moment before anyone broke it.

"I nearly died here," Taunauk said. "Of all the realms, I feel that this was the closest I came to death."

"Lingering death," Shawn added.

"I nearly failed," Taunauk added, ignoring Shawn.

"But you didn't," Helesys replied.

"Because of you."

Helesys smiled. "Someone once told me to readily accept help from my comrades—to use all the tools I had."

Taunauk nodded, conceding the point.

Shawn said, "A strange trio we've made."

~ ~ ~

Ruins of Memory

Reunited, the three heroes walked through the memory of the Wode. Even beneath the oppressive canopy and towering trees, the air between them felt lighter for it.

Before long, they came to ruins that rose up out of the ground like the spine of something dead and forgotten. And as they walked through rubble, Helesys was overcome with familiarity. It was made of the same dark gray and thick stones as the dungeon—

The Gatehouse.

But this was not that Gatehouse. This lay in even more ruin. There were no rooms to shelter in, no ruined tapestries still hanging, and no poems scrawled on parchment. Yet if Helesys had only her Terran senses, she couldn't have said for certain that this was not the Gatehouse they had come upon so long ago. Some part of her knew this was that same sordid structure—perhaps a shade of things to come. But the rest of her that could sense magic knew it was nothing more than illusion.

Still, it was no accident that the memories had brought them here—back to the first time they heard the tale of the

Gatekeeper and her Wolf Knight before they rose to Queen and King.

Helesys wondered aloud, "Why would it bring us here?"

Shawn shook his head. "Don't think too hard on it. Dreams don't work like that. We left Novissimé. There happened to be a forest there. This is just another forest. These ruins are just a mixing of memory."

Taunauk looked over the scene with hard eyes. "You don't sound so sure of that."

Shawn shrugged. "Like I said, dreams are strange things. There's no use trying to use logic to understand them. It's inferences and coincidence all the way down. Random chance, nothing more."

Helesys stayed silent. She didn't point out that Shawn sounded as if he was trying to convince himself. She tried to imagine that it was coincidence that they came upon the ruins of the Gatehouse at such a time, but she did not for a second think it was true.

She looked over the stones, doubt growing within her. For the last realms, the castle had appeared as dark—so black it blotted out the night sky. But these stones looked almost innocent in comparison.

They looked over the ruins warily, both expecting trouble and hoping for clues. At first, they found neither. More and more, Helesys thought back to the inexorable passage of time that ground down all things, even those trapped in the dungeon. Even these monuments to the Queen—ground down to nothing. Not even the statue of the Gatekeeper remained here.

Did the Queen remember what she once was?

Was she the monster that crawled out of the abyss and swallowed gods and worlds? Or was she the benevolent Gatekeeper?

What was she now?

Helesys had so very many questions, and she would keep going until she found the answers.

~

They had been about to leave the ruins when birchmen set upon them. The wooden men appeared between the giant trunks motionless and utterly silent, their bodies contorted in unnatural poses. Helesys searched the treeline, but each time she looked away and looked back, more birchmen filled the gaps between the trees.

And each time she looked back, the birchmen changed. Their once Terran-like bodies grew split and mangled. Faces yawning with insect mandibles, arms broken and hanging, legs split into a dozen fractals.

No matter the transformation, no sound echoed through the forest.

In mere seconds, they were surrounded, and the horde of birchmen had turned into a nightmare. The forest writhed monsters.

Then the twisted birchmen came for them, skittering and slithering with impossible silence.

"Back to back," Taunauk roared. Golden Endroggen sprung from the ether in front of him, rising even quicker than the monsters had. They stretched out to the horde and met them with their own hollow screams.

Shawn tugged the wraps of his arms, and mist cloaked his form. He sprung forward with the speed of a god.

Helesys turned and compounded her power, then slammed the Gar of Shéslang into the ground.

"Siccum putredine."

The poisonous mist of the blight spell rushed out like a dam burst, flooding across her corner of the battlefield, blackening the ground and the base of the trees. Birchmen in its wake crumbled mid-stride and fell to dust, but others leapt up the sides of trees to safety.

The birchmen clinging to the trees writhed, the roots whipping like tentacles as their brethren below died. Then their faces split and a torrent of brown spewed forth—thousands of wooden barbs about to rain down on them.Helesys called on her Ring of Winter and conjured a wall of ice between them. The barrage of needles echoed like rain against the wall.

Behind her, a barbarian roared.

She spared a glance to her allies, and found Taunauk and Shawn holding their own. Golden Endroggen held the field. Taunauk appeared between them and reappeared elsewhere— swapping places with his brethren as fast as he could swing.

And between Helesys and Taunauk, a whole section of battlefield was covered in thin mist, and illuminated with glimmers of light—Shawn moving so fast he appeared only as flickers of death.

Helesys could barely see beyond her comrades' veil of battle, but the birchmen numbers were growing thin.

Helesys turned back to the ice wall and compounded her wand with the spear. Power rattled her arms and her shoulders. She focused on the shadows of birchmen behind the ice and channeled her power into one overwhelming blast.

"Ignis flores!"

Fire *erupted* from her gauntlet. The ice wall exploded with a deafening thundercrack, and fire scoured the forest. Helesys recoiled from the blast. When she looked again, the forest was blackened and shards of ice were embedded up the trunks of nearby trees. Nearly half the battlefield had been sterilized in an instant.

By the time she'd collected herself and turned to help her comrades, they too were slaughtering the last of their wooden enemies.

When Taunauk slew the last birchmen, the golden warriors faded, and Shawn emerged from the mist.

~

Shawn smiled. "That was a good warmup for the main event."

"Agreed," Taunauk said, stowing his shield and battleaxe in his backsling.

The heroes set off deeper into the forest, leaving the carnage of battle behind them.

Helesys asked, "Shawn, what will we find in the center of the dungeon?"

Shawn rubbed his chin. "I don't know, but I would guess that we'll find the castle or something that *looks like* it. Inside, we'll find the Wolf-King's throne."

"Why a castle?" Taunauk asked.

"Why not?" Shawn replied.

"The Queen isn't even Terran," Taunauk said. "The creature is from another world. Who is to say we won't find a hive or something else inhuman?"

Shawn replied, "For whatever reason, a castle seems to be an idea that the Gatekeeper latched onto. Maybe that's what the Wolf King steered her—it—toward." Shawn shrugged. "I know dreams, but I'm only going to be so much help here, I'm afraid."

They came to the edge of the forest. Towering trees gave way to an endless field of golden grasses. The sunset was bleeding red across the sky.

As the three heroes paused at the threshold of the plains, Helesys was overcome with a sense of beauty. She had come so far from Novissimé. Suffered so much. Though her journey wasn't over, she couldn't help but see such a beautiful sunset as a sign.

Was she only feeling that way now that she was so close to the end? Or had she felt the same back then?

This is more than just a memory, Helesys, her wand said. *You felt the sunset was a boon back then, and you feel the same now.*

How did you feel? Helesys asked her wand.

It is an omen of suffering to come. Sunset on an old life.

Helesys replied, *That is what you chose to see.*

It is what happened.

"Helesys…" Taunauk said.

She turned and found her comrades watching her expectantly.

Taunauk asked, "I thought you couldn't talk to your wand anymore?"

Helesys shook her head. "It's just an illusion. Like Shawn said—memory bleeding into reality."

I am always with you, Helesys Byyra.

Helesys ignored her wand and extended her magic sense. The seam of the world—the center of the dungeon—was close.

"Let's go," she said.

~

Helesys, Taunauk, and Shawn walked the field beneath the bleeding sky. She ran metal fingers over the tall brown grasses, taking in their softness.

She knew that these were her last moments of peace.

Apprehension was coming. Helesys felt it crawling across the field like stormclouds, felt the air grow heavy with it. Felt it crawl up her arms and prickle her skin.

Beside her, Taunauk and Shawn walked with weapons drawn. They felt it too.

"We're nearly there, aren't we?" Shawn asked.

But he wasn't talking about the center of the Dungeon. He was talking about the memory…

This was where they found Sala Gahenna.

This was where they were trapped.

Shawn swallowed. "I'm quieter. Faster. I'll scout ahead."

"No," Helesys replied.

Shawn said, "It makes the most sense."

"No," Helesys said again. "This isn't the same…"

Helesys met Shawn's eyes, both wide eyed with realization.

Shawn muttered, "I went ahead that day, and I got trapped first. That can't be… It can't be *why*, can it?"

Helesys thought back to the gallery, to the last time and only time she witnessed this memory. Her and Taunauk had been walking alone. Shawn had already been captured by the Dungeon.

Helesys reached out for her friend. "I'm sorry, Shawn. If we would've know—"

Shawn pulled away. "Don't—just don't. I walked a few paces ahead… And got stuck *in that godsdamn place* by myself. Of all the rotten…" Shawn took a deep breath, then let out a dark laugh. "I should've let you go first, big guy."

Taunauk said nothing. He just stood beside Helesys and waited.

"It doesn't matter now," Helesys said. "We're all together."

"Yeah, but we've been lucky so far," Shawn replied. "If we die, we're going to get split up again. That's if the Wolf King doesn't obliterate us completely or give us a lingering death."

Taunauk stepped forward and laid a heavy hand on Shawn's shoulder. That time, the rogue didn't pull away.

"The path is short and there is no way but forward. We walk it together."

Shawn looked from Taunauk to Helesys, eyes quivering. He nodded. "Just don't leave me."

"We won't," Helesys and Taunauk replied together.

~

The heroes prowled forward, backs together, weapons ready, and eyes feverishly scanning the empty plains.

Their conversation had died and everyone seemed afraid to speak. Afraid to give breath to fate.

Helesys heart pounded in her ears, and her every breath seemed painfully loud.

With each step, her dread grew.

They were close—Helesys knew this. She felt it with every inch of prickled skin and sensitive metal.

Any moment would be their last—

No, Helesys reminded herself. They were not about to be trapped. They were closer to escape.

Her wand whispered, *Helesys… I am afraid.*

There is nothing… But Helesys's thoughts were drowned out. The palpable dread flooded her senses, as if she'd been wading into frigid, murky water and suddenly fallen under. Plunged deep into child-like terror.

Breath caught in her throat, and Helesys was only vaguely aware that she'd stopped walking—paralyzed by fear—and that Taunauk and Shawn were frozen beside her.

The sun was nearly set, and the rolling plains were cast in twilight. The little green of the grass was now gone completely, and the sky was nothing but the last reds of sunset.

And as Helesys stared at the hill, she saw a shimmer—the edge of an illusion. She felt the magic of it, a tingle beneath the numbing dread.

The shimmer stretched out across the hill and rose up as high as she could see into the twilight sky.

A veil.

Helesys stared and tried to peer through the surface. The shimmer looked like waves rolling over an ocean—no. Like blood boiling beneath the skin.

Behind her, Shawn muttered like a scared child, "We're not here. We're not here. We're not here."

Pockets darkened behind the veil—pits where eyes and mouths should be. They gasped open-mouthed against the veil before sinking back inside—the trapped and the damned drowning just beneath the surface and clawing overtop of each other to escape.

"We're not here. We're not here. We're not here."

Just behind the veil.

The dungeon.

"We're not here. We're not here. We're not here."

This was when they were taken.

Helesys kindled power, bolstered it, compounded it with the spear that had pierced a god. Struggled desperately for her rage—for anything else—

All the times she had stood against gods in the mindspace had been a kindness to the dread she felt now. Like a candle in a hurricane.

Any moment now, she would be taken. Lost. Damned.

The veil began to part, and Helesys watched in stunned horror.

There was a gray castle with towering spires set between two mountain peaks. Blue sky above and green forest below.

Novissimé.

"We should go," Shawn muttered. "Anywhere but here."

Helesys reached a hand across Shawn's chest and grabbed his vest. "Wait."

Taunauk stepped beside her, closer than before. "Helesys, we should go through." Faintest tremble in his voice.

"No," she said.

Novissimé was where her journey started, not where it would end.

Helesys reached out with every ounce of power she could muster. She felt for the seam of the world—the heart of the dungeon. Found it.

She screamed as she tore it open.

Novissimé ruptured. The sky and sheer walls of the elven city split in half like torn paper. Frigid darkness spilled out of the seam. It rushed past the heroes and seemed to sweep away the realm.

Helesys pulled harder, and as the world continued to tear open, the heroes saw a new realm beyond—

The jagged gray clouds churned above like shattered glass in a boiling sea. The ground was utterly smooth black glass that reflected nothing. And rising up from it, a castle that stretched up to the sky. The face of it emerged seamlessly from the ground and split into a hundred dagger-point spires, jagged like a nightmare. It looked as if the castle had gutted the sky.

Yet despite the cold, biting air and looming evil, the castle was decidedly finite. Its proportions were nowhere near the titanic visages they'd seen before, nor the sprawling infinite wall. It looked no bigger than Novissimé.

And compared to the prior realms of dreams and illusion, this *felt real.*

"This is it," Helesys said, reassuring herself as much as her comrades. "We're here."

~

They stared at the castle long before anyone spoke. Helesys let the seam close behind them.

"What was that?" Shawn asked. "That was your city back there…"

Beside him, Taunauk mirrored his look of confusion.

"It was an illusion," Helesys replied. "One last trap. They were trying to lead us back to the memory of Novissimé. Back to the beginning of the realm. They meant to trap us in a loop."

Shawn's face wrinkled in disgust. "And they almost got us… again, I think."

Taunauk put a hand on Shawn's shoulder. "No matter what tricks this place has, we're stronger together."

The three shared a smile. Compared to the darkness around them, it was meager—compared to how far they'd come, it was much the same. But it was enough.

Helesys thought back to their escape. "Shawn, back in the garden you said you had a place of respite… but we didn't see your home."

"You saw it."

Helesys's eyes narrowed. "The factory?"
Shawn nodded meekly.
"How could you find respite there?"
The wisp shrugged. "Respite doesn't always look like flowers and sunshine. Some people find solace in mindless toil, sometimes even in sadness. Who says humans and elves are the only species that get to wallow in their misery?"
Taunauk chuckled. "The dream-givers have more right to it than we do."
Shawn mocked his laugh. "Somebody's in a good mood."
"Of course," Taunauk replied. "The end is in sight."

~ ~ ~

NEXT TIME ON

*A BATTLEAXE AND
A METAL ARM*

Book 20:

Empyrean's End

Available November 2022

Spoiler–Free excerpt from *BAMA 20*

"This is it," Helesys said definitively.

The three pressed forward toward the front of the castle. There was an opening in the front wall, some thirty feet square, where a drawbridge or gate might've been. As the heroes passed through, Helesys could feel a raised portion of glass beneath her feet and see the vague outline of seams around the frame.

Moments later, they passed under the gate and the rolling sky above dimmed and died completely. Only the cold followed them.

The heroes found themselves in a long, dark hall. Helesys's mind drifted back to those first rebirths stalking the long hall, full of dread. This passage was an echo of those many memories, except even stranger—there were no sconces, no light sources of any kind, yet Helesys could see clearly. Dim light seemed to emanate from the walls, from everywhere and nowhere, at once. The walls, themselves, were reminiscent of the old bricks, yet they only appeared out of the corner of Helesys's vision—when she looked directly at the wall, the seams faded to smooth purple glass.

The heroes walked in silence; even their footfalls were muted. Taunauk led, Everfall and axe in hand, while Helesys and Shawn followed with power kindled and blades ready. Both the weaver and rogue kept watch behind them.

Together, they pressed forward into the heart of Sala Gahenna.

To be continued November 2022

Thank you for Reading

I hope you enjoyed reading this story as much as I enjoyed writing it.

If you did, I would massively appreciate a short review on Amazon or your favorite book website. Reviews are crucial for any author, and a starred review or even just a line or two can make a huge difference.

It's especially true for the start of a series. Thanks and I hope you enjoy the next one!

Looking for more Engrossing Fantasy?

Check out more stories set in *Eluthiya*—the dark fantasy universe consisting of *A Battleaxe and a Metal Arm*, the ongoing short story collection, *Tales from Another World*, and the monster hunter series, *The Sword of the Gray Queen*.

What questions do you have about *A Battleaxe and a Metal Arm?*

If you've read this far, hopefully you'll read a bit further—both in this book and across the series. I'm not sure how most authors write serials and how much of it is flying by the seat of their pants, but that's not how I do things. For all the major questions that might come up in BAMA, I already have answers for 95% of them. Same goes for the major plot points, twists and climaxes. That might sound boring to some, especially some of you other authors who enjoy variations of writing into the dark, but I think having a solid blueprint is paramount to writing a long series.

So, what questions do you have about the story? Here are a few:

1) ~~What is the dungeon?~~ It's a soul trap of overwhelming size and power. But where did it come from? ~~Is it a force of nature or an ill-made weapon, or perhaps something else entirely?~~ The Dungeon is the Gatekeeper. She is both the marble and the sculptor. In the real world, it looks like a giant cloud with faces writhing just beneath the surface. Helesys speculates

that the reason no one remembers it is because it's so horrific their minds blot it out!

2) ~~Who was Helesys before she got trapped~~? We've learned that Helesys was both a soldier and was the oldest daughter of the elven Great House Byyra.

3) ~~Who was Taunauk before he got trapped~~? There was an omen of a blight in the Endroggen heaven, Accaelum. Taunauk is an Endroggen barbarian who was raised as a warrior and a vessel. His purpose was to one day free the trapped Endroggen souls from the Dungeon.

4) How well did they know each other beforehand?

5) ~~How did Helesys get her metal arm? Likely~~ through injury, amputation, and replacement. She was ~~likely~~ fighting in the Eternal War, the war of the Elves against the Shadowkind.

6) ~~Who is Shawn~~? He is a wisp from the plane of dreams. One who walks through the dreams of elves and humans, while being neither. He has lived as both a god and a mortal. His kind is on the run from the elder god, Nimicus.

7) ~~Why does Shawn feel so familiar to Helesys and Taunauk?~~ They know now that all three of them went to Sala Gahenna together. Though they knew each other only a short while beforehand, it was still enough to bond them inside the dungeon.

Unfortunately, Shawn was captured moments before Helesys and Taunauk, which caused him to be reborn apart from them numerous times.

7) Who is the Wolf King and what sinister plans does he have for our heroes? How did he come to rule over the Dungeon? How does the Gatekeeper factor into all this?

8) Who is the mysterious voice encountered on the white sandy shores of Meridian? Why do they seek the death of the Wolf-King? ...And why did they choose the heroes? The

Voice might be the Gatekeeper... but the truth is still un-known...

Did I miss any questions? Probably. Connect with me and other *BAMA* fans on social media and compare questions!

I've got plans. I've got answers. And I've got them on a drip-feed. Keep reading and expect to find out a little more to the mysteries with each installment. Hopefully, you're as ex-cited about this series as I am.

Connect with the Author

If you want to stay up to date on the latest about Samuel's publishing news and blog, check out his website and consider signing up for his monthly newsletter.

www.SamuelFlemingBooks.com

Samuel can also be found on Reddit, Tiktok, and Facebook.

Samuel Fleming is a Science Fiction and Fantasy author.

He grew up in Maryland, spending most of his time swimming and writing. Swimming gave him a lot of time to daydream, so the two hobbies complemented each other well. Idle day dreams turned into stories, some of which stuck with him for years. These days he swims a little less and writes a lot more.

He loves a good story no matter the medium: Books, TV, video games, comics, tabletop RPG's, or podcasts—most of which he attempts to share with his wife and three kids, and occasionally on his blog.

9 781954 679603